Curious Li'l Lilli

The Lamb With Amazing Grace

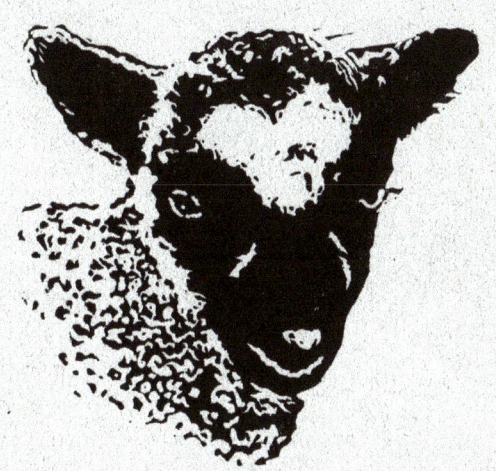

Written by Karlene Kay Ryan

Illustrated by Rich Brimer

Halo Publishing International

Shhhhh!

Listen to the morning. Hear the music of the sun coming over the hill as the light covers the fields with color.

Curious Li'l Lilli 3

Curious

On this bright Spring morning, one curious little lamb hopped and jumped over the sunny field.

Li'l Lilli was sniffing and exploring here and there.

Curious Li'l Lilli   5

Delightful

Li'l Lilli stopped and held perfectly still as the wings of a beautiful butterfly fluttered around her nose.

When it flew away, she chased after it.

Curious Li'l Lilli 7

Overwhelmed

Lilli scampered after the butterfly wondering further and further out into the meadow. Lilli stopped and looked around.

Lilli called out for help, "Baa. Baa Baa!" The Shepherd followed the sound to Lilli asking;
"OK, my curious lamb. Where have you been?"
Then he put his right hand on her head and lead her back to the flock.

Amazed

Later that day, Li'l Lilli was startled as a small animal scurried by her. What was THAT?

Lilli chased after the furry little chipmunk all the way to the edge of the meadow.

Scared

As it got dark and the moon was rising, Lilli heard the yelp of a coyote.

She jumped up and down "Baa! Baa Baa!" Lilli called. The Shepherd, heard her and saw her jumping. He chased the coyote away.

Sensational

As soon as the sun was up the next morning, Lilli was off wondering around. OOPS!—She tripped over a rock and fell into a big flower patch of violets and calla lilies.

She nibbled on a pretty white one and licked her lips. ICKY! Then she turned to the delicious looking purple violets! Li'l Lilli kept eating and eating.

Curious Li'l Lilli   15

Wary and Weary

When she finally had her fill, Lilli tried to stand.
"Baa! Baa Baa!" she cried.

Now, she had a tummy ache.

Hearing her call out, the Shepherd carried the lamb.

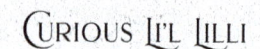

Curious Li'l Lilli 17

Excited

The next morning the sheep all gathered and watched the dawn of the day.

Except for one.

Li'l Lilli had pranced off through the field.

Curious Li'l Lilli   19

Fantastic

The little lamb reached the edge of the grassy meadow where the field met the forest. She followed the creek and found a big green frog sitting on a rock deep into the forest.

"Ribbit! Ribbit!" said the frog, and he jumped away. Curious, Lilli leaped after him.

Frightened

The little lamb could not keep up with the frog. Lilli realized that she was lost very deep in the woods.

"Baa! Baa Baa!" she cried, but no one came.

She ran back through the trees, this way and that way. Soon, the woods grew dark and Lilli could no longer see. Scared, the little lamb sought shelter under a fallen tree.

Lost

Night fell and the Shepherd walked by his sheep when he discovered he was missing a little lamb. "Li'l Lilli," called the Shepherd. "Lilli!"

The Shepherd looked for his lamb throughout the night.

**By the creek.
Under a log.
Behind the rocks.**

Found

Hours passed. As dawn broke, sunlight peeked through the tops of the trees. The Shepherd never wavered in his search for Lilli. He knew he would find her. "Lilli!" he called again. "Li'l Lilli!"

From under the tree, the little lamb heard her Shepherd's voice and cried out, "Baa!—Baa Baa!"

He rushed through the trees, following the sound of her voice and found Li'l Lilli huddled under the tree in the leaves and twigs.

The Shepherd brushed the branches from her coat. He gently patted Li'l Lilli to ease her fears.

"Baa!—Baa Baa!"

Safe

The Shepherd gathered Little Lilli Lamb in his arms and held her where she was safe—close to his heart.

He gave her a hug of love and carried her with joy, back to the big, green pasture.

References

"He tends his flock lie a shepherd He gathers the lambs in his arms and carries them close to his heart." Isaiah: 40:11

"For I the Lord your God hold your right hand; I am the Lord, Who says to you, 'fear not; I will help you.'" Isaiah: 41:13

"I am the Good Shepherd: and I know and recognize My own, and My own know and recognize My voice, and they follow me." John: 10:14

"In Your presence is fullness of joy, at Your right hand there are pleasures forevermore." Psalm 16:11

"Though he falls, he shall not be utterly cast down, for the Lord grasps his hand in support and upholds him." Psalm 37:24

"My whole being follows hard after You and clings closely to You. Your right hand upholds me." Psalm 63:8

"If I take wings of the morning or dwell in the uttermost parts of the sea, even there shall Your hand will lead me, and Your right hand shall hold me." Psalm: 73:23

"He will feed His flock like a shepherd: He will gather the lambs in His arms. He will carry them in His bosom and will gently lead those that have their young." Isaiah: 41:10

"The Lord is my Shepherd to guide and shield me. He makes me to lie down in green pastures. He leads me beside the still and restful waters." Psalm 23:1–2

"Says the Lord: I will search for My sheep. I will rescue them out of the places where they have been scattered. I will feed them with good pasture. I will seek that which was lost and bring back that which has strayed." Ezekiel 34:11–16

All biblical passages from:
Amplified Bible; Zondervan Bibles

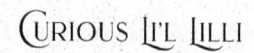

Curious Li'l Lilli

Copyright ©2022 Karlene Kay Ryan
Illustrations ©2022 Rich Brimer

All rights reserved.
No part of this book may be reproduced in any manner whatsoever without the prior written permission of the publisher, except in the case of brief quotations embodied in reviews.

ISBN: 978-1-63765-033-2
LCCN: 2021909033

Halo Publishing International, LLC
www.halopublishing.com

Printed and bound in the United States of America.

Dedication

Timothy, Erin, Keely, Lauren, Renee, Genevieve, Seamus, Cara Rose and Kai.

CPSIA information can be obtained
at www.ICGtesting.com
Printed in the USA
LVHW011641020322
712263LV00002BA/5